Johnny's Dragon

"I'm a dragon," hissed the little black creature. "I've run away because I'm so small, and my wings are so tiny I can't fly, and I've only got one head."

"Is that bad?" asked Johnny.

"It is for a dragon," hissed the little dragon. "All the other dragons at my school have three heads, so they're always teasing me."

Johnny had his own problems at school, so he knew what the little dragon meant. But somehow sharing them made them go away and when the dragon had to leave they were both much happier.

A touching and relevant story for 5-8 year olds.

Johnny's Dragon

by
Irina Korschunow
Pictures by
Mary Rahn

Translated from the German
by Anthea Bell

Hippo Books
Scholastic Publications Limited
London

Scholastic Publications Ltd,
141–143 Drury Lane, London, WC2B 5TG, England

Scholastic Book Services,
50 West 44th Street, New York, NY 10036, USA

Scholastic Tab Publications Ltd,
123 Newkirk Road, Richmond Hill, Ontario L4C 3G5
Canada

H J Ashton Co Pty Ltd, Box 579,
Gosford, New South Wales, Australia

H J Ashton Co Pty Ltd,
9–11 Fairfax Avenue, Penrose, Auckland, New Zealand

First published by Deutsche Taschenbuch Verlag 1978
First published in Great Britain by
Scholastic Publications Ltd 1982

Made and printed in the USA
Set in Plantin Roman

Contents

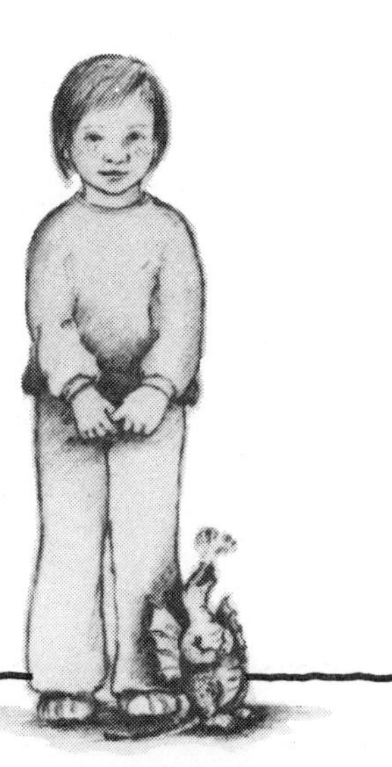

Johnny Alone

"Come on, Johnny, get up!" said Johnny's mother. "Time to go to school!"

Johnny crawled out of bed very, very slowly. He washed his face and cleaned his teeth very, very slowly. He didn't want to go to school. And he had been looking forward to it so much, too. But Simon Hall had shouted, "Fatty!" and "Podge!" at him the very first day, and ever since Johnny had been afraid of going to school. He wanted to stay at home, but that wasn't allowed.

"Have a nice day!" said Johnny's mother, and he set off for school very, very slowly. He walked down the road and through the park. He crossed the school playground and went into his classroom.

"Here comes old Fatty Podge!" yelled Simon Hall. Some of the children laughed, and Simon pushed Johnny. Johnny wanted to push him back, but he didn't dare. Simon was stronger, and he had lots of friends, while Johnny didn't have any friends at all. He sat at his desk feeling angry and sad. He was so sad he couldn't pay attention to the lesson.

"Wake up, Johnny!" said Miss Benson. "It's your turn to read."

Johnny jumped. When he read, he stumbled over the words and got them all mixed up. The children laughed again, and Miss Benson said, "Night is the time for dreaming, you know, Johnny!"

Johnny's sums came out wrong too, and he didn't even feel like painting. It's no good, he thought. I can't do anything.

The games lesson was worst of all. Johnny couldn't run as fast as the others, and he never got his hands on the ball.

"Old Fatty Podge is so heavy he can't even pick his feet up!" said Simon Hall.

No, Johnny never wanted to go to school again.

The Little Dragon

Johnny trudged miserably through the park on his way home. There was a bench under the big beech tree, and he sat down on it. It was cold, but he didn't mind. He picked up a twig and drew lines and squiggles and circles on the sandy path. Then he saw something. One of the circles was turning into a head! Not a picture of a head. A real live head came popping up out of the ground. A little black head with a nose and a red tongue, and puffs of dark smoke were coming out of its nostrils.

"Hullo," said the little black head. It made a funny hissing sound when it talked. "Who are you? You're the funniest looking dragon I've ever seen in my life!"

"Dragon?" said Johnny. "I'm not a dragon.

I'm a human being!"

The little black head puffed out another small cloud of smoke.

"A real human being?"

"Of course," said Johnny. "And what are you?"

"What am I?" The little black head wagged back and forth. "Can't you guess?"

Then Johnny saw the creature's body. It had a tummy and a back, two wings and a long tail and four big paws. It was black all over, and no bigger than a guinea pig.

"I'm a dragon!" hissed the little black creature. "I come from Dragonland. That's quite a long way off."

"Well, what are you doing here?" asked Johnny.

The little dragon looked round, cautiously. Then he whispered, "I've run away because I'm so small, and my wings are so tiny I can't even fly, and I've only got one head!"

"Is that bad?" asked Johnny.

"It is, for a dragon," hissed the little dragon. "You see, all the other dragons at my school have three heads, so they're always teasing me."

1
2
3

He stopped for a moment. Then he asked, "Can I come and stay with you? I could live in that thing."

"That's my satchel," said Johnny. "I take it to school with me."

"School? You mean human beings go to school too?" hissed the little dragon in surprise. "I thought Dragonland was the only place they had schools! Dragons learn how to breathe fire at our school. One head breathes red fire, the second head breathes yellow fire, and the third head breathes blue fire."

"But all you're breathing out is smoke," said Johnny.

"That's because I've only got one head. What do you learn at your school?"

"Reading and writing and sums," said Johnny.

"Can you do all those things?" hissed the little dragon.

Johnny didn't answer.

"Will you take me to see your school?" asked the little dragon.

Johnny still didn't answer.

"Oh, please take me!" begged the little

dragon.

"Well, we'll have to go home first," said Johnny. He opened his satchel, and the little dragon jumped in.

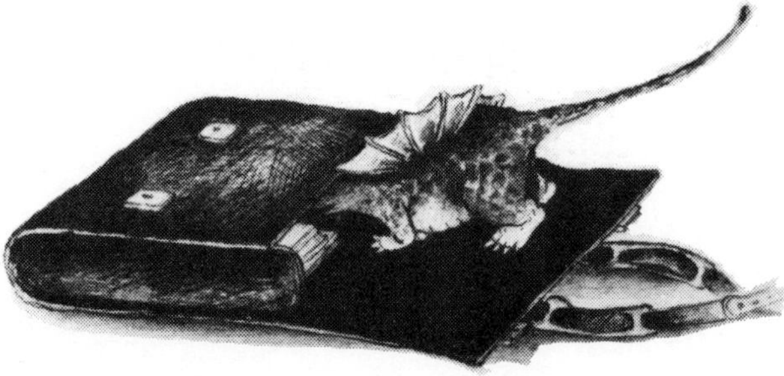

Chocolate-flavoured Fire

When Johnny got home his Granny was waiting on the steps.

"Here's a present for you, Johnny," said Granny, and she gave him a bar of chocolate.

Johnny went into his own room, and the little dragon hopped out of the satchel.

"What's that?" he asked. "That nice warm thing?"

"It's a fire," said Johnny. "We still have real fires in the fireplaces in our house."

"Fire?" hissed the little dragon. "Oh, I'm so glad I met you! I want some fire to eat. Please – I'm starving! Quick!"

Johnny picked the little dragon up and held him close to the fire. The dragon stuck his head into the flames. He slurped and he smacked his lips and he wagged his tail.

"Don't you like eating fire too?" he asked Johnny.

"Eating fire?" Johnny laughed. "Human beings don't eat fire!"

"What do you like eating, then?" asked the little dragon.

"Things like chocolate," said Johnny. He took the wrapper off his bar. "My Granny gives me chocolate almost every day. Want a piece?"

The little dragon shook his head. "But could you put a piece on the fire for me?" he asked. "I'd love to try chocolate-flavoured fire!"

Johnny broke off two pieces of chocolate and put them on the fire, and the little dragon stuck his head into the flames again.

"Fantastic! Chocolate-flavoured fire tastes lovely!" he hissed. "More, please! More!"

He kept asking for more until Johnny had put his whole bar of chocolate on the fire.

"Oh well, I expect Granny will give me some more," said Johnny.

"Yes, yes!" hissed the little dragon. "Then I can eat chocolate-flavoured fire all day long." He stood on his hind legs and began to prance and dance about. "This is the way dragons dance for joy," he said proudly.

Johnny thought of a song, and he sang it to the little dragon.

Dragons eat some funny food.
They seem to think that fire tastes good!
And then, if they can ever get a
Chocolate fire it's even better!

"What's that you were doing?" asked the little dragon.

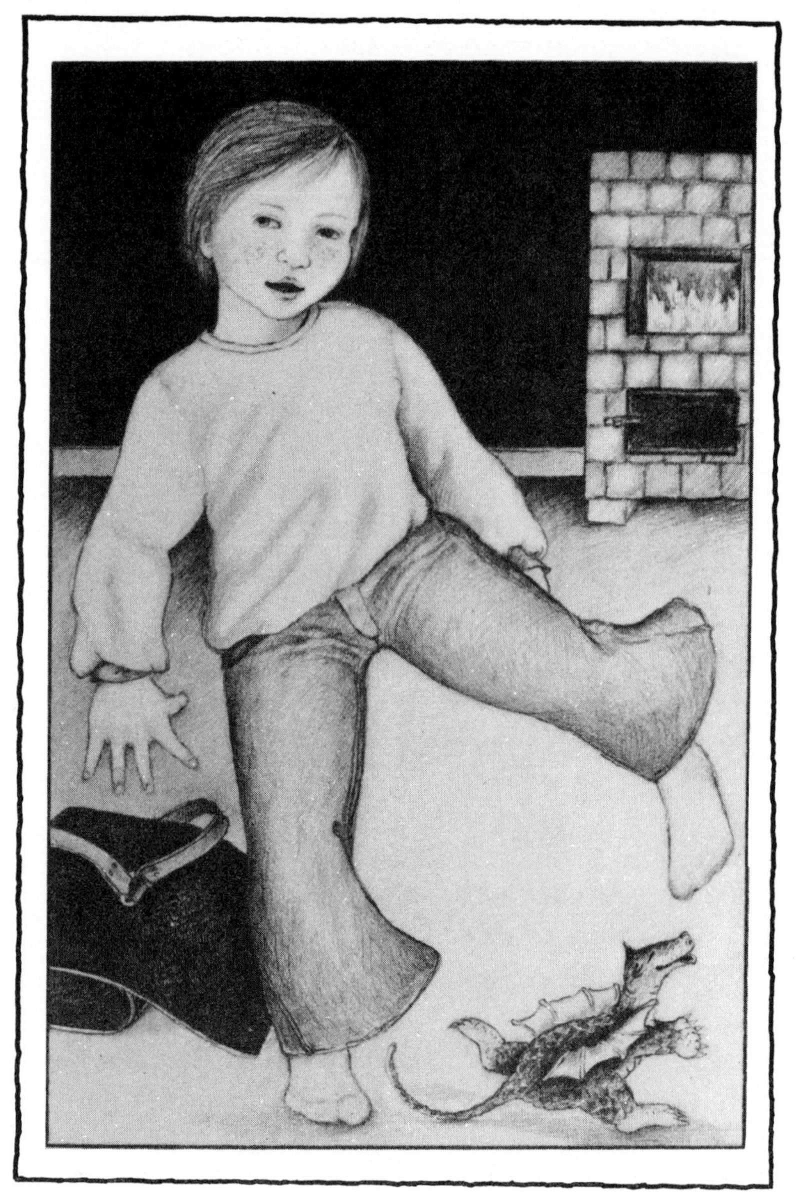

"It's called singing," said Johnny.

"You sing very nicely," said the little dragon.

Johnny shook his head. "Simon Hall says I can't sing in tune," he said.

The dragon puffed out a little cloud of smoke. "Simon Hall is silly!" he said. "Sing me that song again! Please!"

So Johnny sang his song again, and the little dragon sang too and danced round in a circle. Johnny started dancing as well. He felt so good that he even turned a somersault.

"What was that?" asked the little dragon.

"A somersault!" said Johnny. "And I've never been able to turn a somersault before because I'm too fat!"

"I want to turn somersaults!" hissed the little dragon. So Johnny went head over heels again, and the little dragon copied him. "I may only have one head," he hissed, "but I've learnt to sing and I've learnt to turn somersaults! How surprised the other dragons will be!"

The Little Dragon Goes to School

Next morning, Johnny took the little dragon to school with him.

"Out of my way, Fatty!" said Simon Hall, pushing Johnny.

"Go on, push him back!" whispered the little dragon, through a crack in the satchel. But Johnny didn't dare.

"Get your exercise books out," said Miss Benson. "We're going to do some writing."

She wrote on the board, "The hare has long ears." The children had to copy it. But Johnny couldn't stop thinking about Simon calling him Fatty, and he got the letters all wrong and wobbly.

At break, Johnny went and stood in a corner of the playground. He had his satchel with him, and the little dragon stuck his head out. "I don't like that boy Simon!" he hissed. "He reminds me of some of the dragons in my class at school. The ones who teased me!"

"Did you tease them back?" asked Johnny.

"No," said the little dragon. "I didn't dare."

They both thought for a bit. Then the little dragon said, "But Simon isn't very clever. He said you couldn't sing in tune! Perhaps he isn't really very strong either, and if you fight back he might run away."

"I don't think he would," said Johnny.

"Well, have a go!" said the little dragon. "THEN I'd feel brave enough to have a go too."

The bell rang, and Johnny went back into the classroom.

"Here comes old Fatty Podge!" shouted Simon Hall. He pushed Johnny again.

But Johnny picked up his satchel, put it in front of him, and pushed Simon hard with it. Simon sat down on the floor very suddenly.

"Ow!" he yelled. "Fatty Podge pushed me!"

Johnny was afraid of Simon's friends, but none of them moved.

"It serves you right!" said Susie Jones. "I'm glad Johnny pushed you back."

Simon went and sat down at his desk, and he didn't say anything at all.

The Little Dragon Learns to Write

The little dragon was lying in front of the fire while Johnny did his homework. He had to write out, "The hare has long ears," five times.

The first time, he wrote, "The hair has lon ears."

The second time, he wrote, "Th har has loong eres."

The third time, he wrote, "The are has lung eares."

Johnny's mother looked at his exercise book and shook her head. "Dear me, Johnny, that won't do," she said. "You'd better start again."

Johnny chewed the end of his pen.

"It's no good," he said out loud. "I can't do it."

"Can't do what?" asked the little dragon.

"Can't write properly," said Johnny.

The little dragon jumped up on the table.

"How do you do writing?" he asked. "Show me how!"

Johnny wrote "The hare" in his exercise book. "You ought to be glad you don't have to learn to write!" he said.

The little dragon picked up a pencil and a piece of paper. "Show me again, so I can do it too," he hissed.

Johnny wrote first one letter, then another, and then another. At last he said, "That says 'The hare'. "

"The hare," repeated the little dragon, copying all the letters on his own piece of paper. "Look, we can write that beautifully! What comes next?"

" 'Has,' " said Johnny.

"Has," wrote the little dragon over and over again on his piece of paper, until it looked right. Then he learned how to write "long" and "ears" too.

"We can both write very beautifully!" said the little dragon proudly.

Then Johnny's mother came into the room.

The hare
has long
ears.
The Hare has long Ears
A+

"Oh, well done, Johnny," she said.

"What about me?" asked the little dragon, when she had gone out again.

"Well done you too!" said Johnny.

The little dragon sat on Johnny's exercise book and made up a song:

I'm a dragon who can write!
Isn't that a funny sight?
As dragons go, I may be small,
But the rest of them can't write at all!

The Little Dragon Draws a Picture

Johnny and the little dragon were sitting on Johnny's bed, and the little dragon was telling Johnny about Dragonland.

"I've got a dragon father there, and a dragon mother, and – "

Then he found a box of coloured crayons.

"Are these for eating?" he asked.

"No," said Johnny, "they're for drawing pictures." He pointed to a picture over his bed. "I once drew that, when I was in nursery school," he said.

"You draw lovely pictures!" hissed the little dragon.

Johnny shook his head.

"Simon Hall says my pictures are just silly blobs of colour," he said.

The little dragon looked at the crayons. "I wish I could draw pictures," he said. "Please show me how!"

"No," said Johnny. "I don't feel like drawing pictures any more."

The little dragon rubbed his head against Johnny's leg. "Don't be like that!" he begged. "I want to draw pictures so much!"

And he went on and on, until Johnny fetched his drawing pad and scribbled some lines and squares and circles on the top sheet of paper.

"That's not a real picture," hissed the little dragon. "Show me how to draw real pictures!"

"But I can't," said Johnny. "Oh, well – what do you want me to draw, then?" he asked.

"Me!" hissed the little dragon.

Johnny looked at the little dragon and began to draw. He drew the dragon's head and tummy and back and tongue.

"Is that me?" asked the little dragon. "Is it really me?"

He picked up some of the crayons and he drew, too. First he drew a little circle, and

then a big fat circle with two lines sticking out of it. "That's you," he told Johnny. "Do you like my picture?"

"You forgot my legs," said Johnny.

"You forgot mine too," said the little dragon. "I know what! Let's go on drawing till we've both done really good pictures. Would you like to do that?"

Johnny said yes, because he could see how much the little dragon wanted him to, and they spent all afternoon drawing. They drew lots of brightly coloured pictures, and they hung the two best over Johnny's bed. Johnny's picture showed the little dragon sitting in front of the stove eating chocolate fire. And the little dragon's picture showed Johnny putting gingerbread in the flames to make him some gingerbread fire.

"We can both draw lovely pictures," said the little dragon happily, and he breathed out three little puffs of black smoke.

The Little Dragon Climbs a Tree

Johnny and the little dragon had been playing tag in the garden.

"I'm tired!" hissed the little dragon, and he sat down under the apple tree.

Johnny sat down beside him. The sun was shining, and winter was almost over.

"What a big tree!" said the little dragon. "I wish I could climb this tree. Show me how!"

"I can't climb trees," said Johnny.

"I don't believe you," hissed the little dragon. "I expect that's something else silly old Simon Hall told you. Come on!"

Slowly, Johnny got to his feet, grabbed a branch and hauled himself up. The little dragon climbed up after him.

"This is easy!" he hissed.

They climbed on, from branch to branch. Johnny was puffing and panting and muttering to himself. The little dragon was out of breath too. But at last they reached the top. From the top of the tree, they could see the balcony of the house next door, and Mrs Jackson next door standing on her balcony scratching her nose.

"I'm higher up than any dragon in the world!" hissed the little dragon happily, "even if I am the smallest dragon of all, and I only have one head! When I get back to Dragonland I'm not going to let the others tease me any more!"

Then he looked down. "You know, we really are rather a long way up," he hissed. "How do we get down again?"

"I don't know," said Johnny.

"I'm scared," hissed the little dragon, and suddenly he began to cry. "N . . . now I'll h-have to stay up here for – for always!" he sobbed. "I won't ever have ch-chocolate f-fire to eat again!"

Johnny hated to hear the little dragon cry. He put him in his pocket. "Don't cry," he said. “I’ll try climbing down.”

But it was no good. The tree was too tall.

Then Johnny’s father came home. He stood underneath the tree and told Johnny what to do. “You must put your foot on that branch,” he said. “And now that one. That’s the idea. Well done! And next time you climb a tree, just remember you have to climb down again!”

Johnny nodded. He had climbed quite enough trees for one day. But the little dragon immediately forgot that he had been so frightened he had cried.

“Climbing trees is fun!” he hissed. “Let’s climb more trees tomorrow!”

The Little Dragon Reads a Story

The little dragon had been living with Johnny for quite a long time now, and he had learnt all sorts of things. He wanted to learn to read too.

"Reading is boring," said Johnny. "It takes at least an hour to read just one page."

"You've got a big fat book with coloured pictures on your bookshelf," hissed the little dragon. "What's inside it?"

"Stories," said Johnny.

The little dragon puffed a little round cloud of smoke into the air.

"I wish I was a dragon who could read stories," he said. And he wouldn't stop pestering Johnny. Out in the street, he stopped in front of every advertisement and

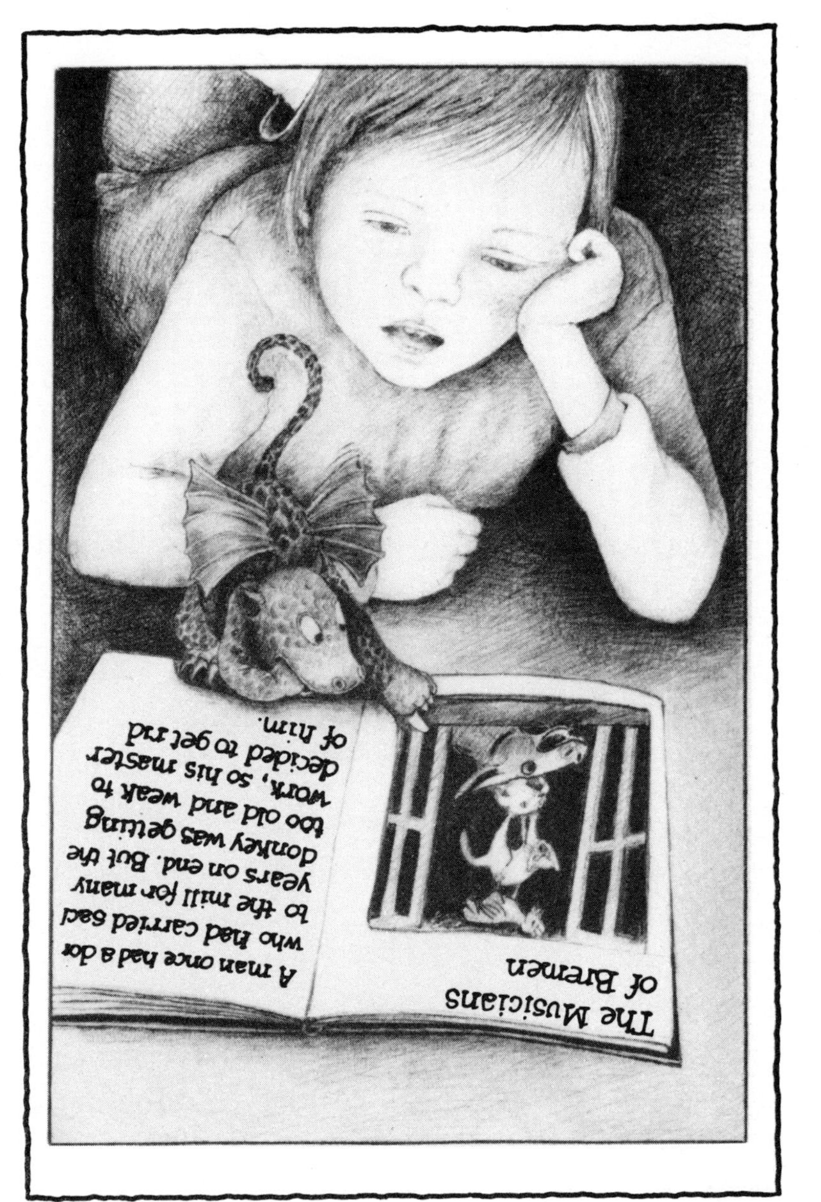
The Musicians
of Bremen
A man once had a do
who had carried sac
to the mill for many
years on end. But the
donkey was getting
too old and weak to
work, so his master
decided to get rid
of him.

outside every shop, and asked, "What's that letter? What does this word say? Please read it to me!"

Soon the little dragon could read all sorts of difficult words, like CHEMIST and LAUNDERETTE and SUPERMARKET.

And one day he took the story book out of the bookshelf, sat on Johnny's lap and began to read. "The Mu - mu - "

"The Mu-si-cians of Bremen," said Johnny.

"Good!" said the little dragon. "The Musicians of Bremen. Go on!"

They enjoyed the story so much that they didn't stop until they had read two whole pages.

"We can both read stories now," hissed the little dragon. "I'd better make up a song about it!

Dragons can't read books.
Or that's how it looks!
But I have just read one . . .

He stopped. "I don't know how to finish it," he hissed.

" '*And so has my friend John,*' " said Johnny, laughing.

"John?" The little dragon shook his head. "That's not your name."

"It's near enough," said Johnny.

Summer Is Coming

"Get up, Johnny," said Johnny's mother. "Time to go to school!"

Out of doors, the sun was shining, and Johnny's mother said at breakfast, "Summer is coming! We won't need to light the fires any more now."

"Here comes old Fatty!" shouted Simon Hall when he saw Johnny. But Johnny didn't mind any more.

"Fatty Podge!" shouted Simon again.

"Simon Hall looks pretty small!" said Johnny.

The little dragon laughed himself sick, and the other children laughed too.

"You know what?" said Susie Jones. "Johnny isn't at all fat now, and Simon never noticed!"

Then Miss Benson came in. "We're going to do some reading," she said.

Susie Jones started, and Johnny was next. He read five sentences and he only made one mistake.

"Very good, Johnny!" said Miss Benson. Johnny felt pleased, because he could read, and because he wasn't fat any more, and because it was so much more fun at school now.

Susie Jones came over to him at break.

"It's my birthday on Friday," she said. "Will you come to my party? Andy and Mary and Louise are coming too."

Johnny felt more pleased than ever. He wondered what to give Susie for a birthday present.

"I'm still here, Johnny," hissed the little dragon.

Johnny patted his head. "I know you are," he said.

But he was thinking about the birthday party.

Johnny Is Not Alone

School was over, and Johnny and the little dragon were going home. When they came to the bench underneath the beech tree, Johnny sat down. The little dragon lay at his feet.

"I had another dream about Dragonland last night," he said.

"Did you?" asked Johnny.

"It was a lovely dream," hissed the little dragon. Then neither of them said anything for some time.

At last the little dragon said, "I'm hungry! What's for my dinner? Is there chocolate-flavoured fire or gingerbread-flavoured fire today?"

"I'm afraid there isn't anything," said Johnny. "Now that winter's over my mother

won't be lighting the fires."

"No fires?" hissed the little dragon. "Are you sure?"

Johnny nodded his head. "And what's more, my Granny noticed me putting chocolate on the fire, so she's stopped giving me any!"

The little dragon rested his head on his front paws and sighed heavily.

"Come on," said Johnny at last. "Time to go home."

But the little dragon did not move.

"No," he hissed quietly.

"What's the matter?" asked Johnny.

"I'm not coming home with you," said the little dragon. "I'm going back to Dragonland. I don't think the others will tease me now. After all, I'm the only dragon in the world who can read! And I can sing, and write, and draw pictures, and I can climb trees and turn somersaults! So not having three heads won't matter any more."

"Oh, please don't go!" cried Johnny.

The little dragon looked at him and blinked his eyes hard.

"I had a lovely time staying with you," he said. "But I'm a dragon, and I belong in Dragonland. Just pat my head once more, will you?"

Johnny leaned down, and suddenly he realized that his fingers were patting the sandy path. The little dragon had disappeared. There was nothing there at all but lines and circles in the sand.

"Oh, little dragon!" cried Johnny. But there was no answer.

Then he went home, through the park and up the road. He felt sad without the little dragon in his satchel.

A new shop had just opened on the corner, and there was a beautiful shell in its window.

Johnny stopped.

"That's a nice shell," he said to himself. "I know! I'll give Susie Jones that shell for her birthday."

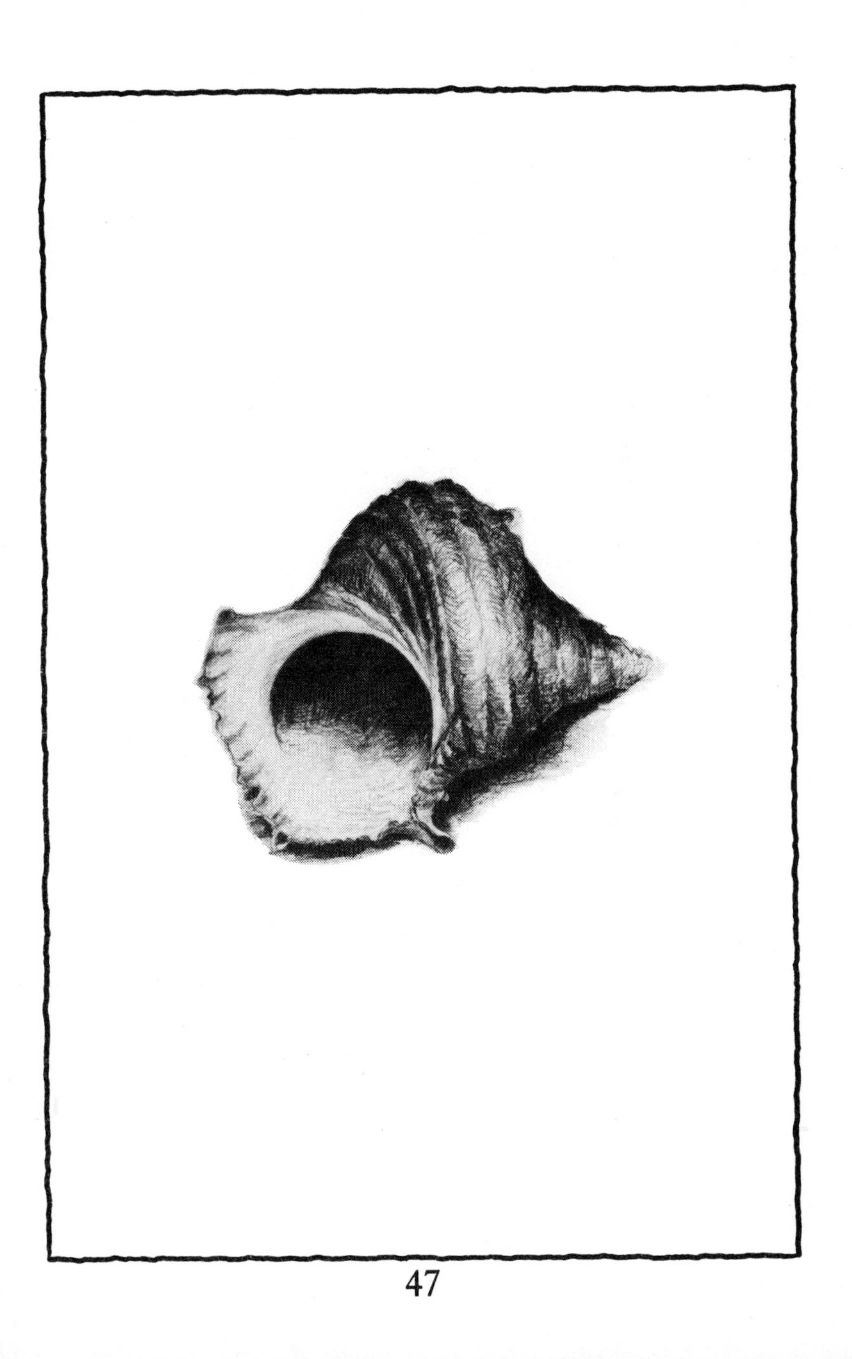